Liberated Publishing Inc

Presents…

Sensual Delights

Fantasies Of A Poet

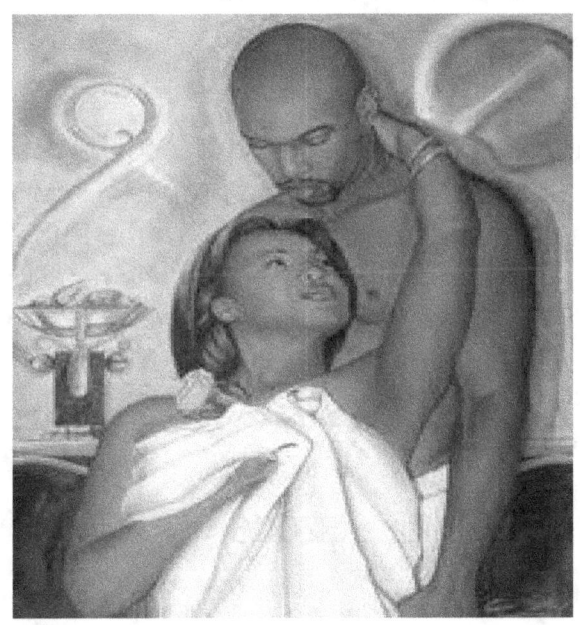

Liberated Publishing Inc.
1860 Wilma Rudolph Bvd
Clarksville, TN 37040

© 2005 Richard "Reason" Garrett

Published by: Liberated Publishing Inc

ISBN 978-0982552322

First Printing: March 2006

Printed in the United States of America

This book was dedicated to
My one and only
Sunshine
Who has been my inspiration

Acknowledgements

First off let me thank God because without him none of this would even be possible.

I can't thank my friends and family enough for hanging in there with me during the process off writing and publishing this book. It took quite a while but it finally happened.

To all the cool peoples I met online who took the time to read a few excerpts from my book and gave me feed back, thanks for your support.

To all my fellow inmates who kept it real with me and supported me from day one when I began this novel, I gots nothing but love for ya'll. Special shot outs to the B&B Fam Liberated Publishing staff, Spellbound Entertainment, Storm, King Pen, Clay, Jay Rize, Lil D, Peppers, Kryme Deezy, my human dictionary a.k.a Sparks, my multi talented cousin T.K a.k.a. Da Truth. Ya'll boys' keep ya'll heads up and know I haven't forgot about you.

Last but definitely not least I want to send a special thanks to my inspiration, my voice, and my reason for even taking on this project. Sunshine your love and support has carried me through some very difficult times. I am forever grateful for God allowing you to have been apart of my life.

Prologue

Dear Sunshine,

Night after night your name rings in my head like an endless melody, as I lie here wishing you were here next to me, while I share your warmth and hold you close, I guess you can say that's what I miss most. Damn my life seemed to be one huge mess, even before the tragic night of my arrest. It all began when I decided to put love on hold, hardening my heart until it formed a stone mold, leaving me hollow inside with barely a glimmer of hope, that I tried filling with hood dreams of getting rich slangin' dope, along with smoking and drinkin' just to numb the pain, but like an umbrella with big holes it couldn't keep out the rain. Empty and incomplete is how I felt inside, things just weren't the same without you by my side, from your smile and laugh to your frown and tears, images engraved in my mind through all these years, haunting me in ways you'll never know, even in my darkest moments your sweet memory brightly glows, illuminating the deepest depths of my soul, uncovering hidden feelings that had yet to be told, but no longer as I try to break the silence, hoping to recapture time in all its vibrance, making it linger in my mind as long as I can, sorting through fact and fiction so I can truly understand, with memories and fantasies merging at one time, as my pen touches down on this pad line after line, absorbing the scene as an escape from reality, fighting off the depression that makes it an abnormality, as I pour out my soul surrounded by 3 walls, with a cage in front of me standing tall, along with many other barriers that keep me caged in, separating me from the outside world that I spent days in. I think back to all those times I took for granted, instead of enjoying what

I had I moved around too frantic, trying to get my hands on bigger and better things, while chasing after ill inspired dreams, losing sight of original priorities, now I look back regretfully…

Sincerely yours,

The Saga Begins

Dear Sunshine,

Who would have thought that the warmth of your smile would reach the depths of my soul, unthawing the ice around my heart that made me so cold, but I aint even gonna front like it was love at first sight, cuz the only thing on my mind was hittin' it that night. Though it was years ago I still remember how we first met. I was a complete asshole but at that age what did you expect. We were at the bus stop dressed in blue jeans and white tees, mine's baggy while yours fits nice and tightly. The official uniform for those in Alternative School, the place students go when expelled for actin' a fool. Across from the school is where we wait on the city bus, while niggas show their true colors wild'n out all around us. Through the mayhem I manage to catch sight of you, as my eyes scope out your body that stands no taller than 5'2, with light honey golden brown skin, and alluring eyes that draw me in, to the point where now I'm only a few feet away, as I approach I overhear your friend ask "So how was your day?" Before you can reply I ask for a moment of your time, you reply with a smile and say "Sure I don't mind." After pulling you to the side we engage in that introductory conversation, until the bus pulls up to take us to the transit station, where we switch buses to the one that serves the North side, as we sit next to each other conversing the whole ride. Everything was going smooth until we're about 5 minutes from your crib, that's when I get straight to the point and ask, "So what's the biz?" With an attitude you say, "What the fuck ya mean by that?" Followed by "I aint no fuckin' hoe I don't get down like that!" Me not giving a fuck I reply "Mayne whateva trick. Why you frontin' like you aint tryin to hop on this dick?" For the rest of our convo

3

you proceed to cuss me out, until we reach your stop then you flip me off as the door opens to let you out. As the bus pulls off I think to myself "Mayne she can go to hell, sheeit if she won't give it up I know someone else who will." But somewhere in my subconscious I store your memory away, along with the hope that our paths will cross again someday…

To be continued

Sincerely yours,

The Saga Continues

Dear Sunshine,

Its funny how life can make opposites attract, ever notice the relationships between fiction and fact, or between love and hate. Without both extremes how could we appreciate all the things about each other that bring us pleasure, and all the memories that we've grown to treasure, both good and bad I'll keep with me always, as I look forward to creating more one of these days. But for now the past has got my attention, as I continue our story that begins with fate's intervention. On a Saturday night me and my boys go cop a dub, roll up and smoke as we ride out to the club. A teen club that is which happens to be hosting its quarterly slumber party, that is guaranteed to be thick with females showin' off their bodies, which is the main reason why we decided to come, plus the legit excuse to be out all night having fun. As we pull into the parking lot of Club 24/7, we all take turns blowin' shotguns to keep our minds in the heavens. Then skip the long line cuz we in good with the staff, while the haters make faces like they got sticks up their ass. Once inside we meet up with the rest of the crew at our post up spot, while the females on the dance floor drop it like it's hot. After kickin' it for a while I decide to go where the action is, as I hit the dance floor lookin' to spit the biz, my eyes somehow find you through the crowd. Damn, after 2 years I can't believe I'm seeing you now. For the most part you still look the same, with the exception of added curves to your short frame. Before I realize it I'm headed in your direction, with that subconscious hope overriding my previous rejection. As I approach your eyes widen in surprise, then quickly glare at me as if you're plotting my demise. Wanting to defuse the situation I sincerely apologize, then lead the way as we step outside. Now that we're away from the boisterous atmosphere, I no longer have to yell in your ear, as we carry on a civil conversation, with us both agreeing to forget that ugly situation, and put forth the effort to get to know each other, as we walk back in after having exchanged numbers.

To be continued…

Sincerely yours,

The Saga Continues Part 2

Dear Sunshine,

Destiny can be a very strange thing, you never know what fate may bring, but I believe fate brought us together for a reason, making it a law that if broken would be high treason. After conversing on the phone for several weeks, all I can focus on is the next time we're gonna meet. With us going to different schools and me working two jobs that don't leave us much time, not to mention on the low-key tip I stay on the grind. So when you agreed last night to skip school today. I went to sleep that night with a smile on my face. Awakening bright and early while fresh dew still lies on the grass, with a wet glaze covering each house I pass. As I pull up to your house all is calm except for the birds singing, and the fresh moist breeze that the morning sky is bringing. Slowly approaching the door I notice even the inside seems quiet. Mayne I know you didn't renege after I was practically invited. Naw that can't be cuz you called this morning with instructions, saying the door would be unlocked and to just come right in. Without any further thought I grab the cold moist doorknob and open it, then cautiously call your name as if it were the first time I've ever spoken it. After repeating your name this time more confidently, with no response I begin to wonder where could you be, as I slowly move through the living room and into the kitchen in my search to find you, I peek out onto the back porch and take in the suburban view, then thinking I heard a noise I break from my gazing, smiling to myself at this hide and seek game you're playing. As I head down the hallway towards the bedrooms that are the last area of the house to hide, I take a quick peek into your mom's room even though I know you won't be inside. Moving on towards your room where surely you must be, I pause at the bathroom and hear absolutely nothing, but I do feel a warmth like a summer breeze reach out and fill my body from head to toe, along with the sweet fragrance of a freshly cut rose. Better yet make that a garden full of fresh flowers in full bloom, as I think to myself that you just retreated from a hot steamy shower back to your room. After lingering for a moment I creep toward your room where I figured I'd find my radiant queen, perhaps lying upon her bed but wearing what kind of clothing? Slowly grabbing the knob and turning it so as to not make a sound. In I go… nothing… you're nowhere to be found. Then I feel that warmth spilling from the bathroom as it drifts through the air, causing me to come to the conclusion that you must be in there. Turning around I catch the scent of a warm sweet vanilla sugar fragrance, that seems to entice me to follow with its intentions being flagrant. As I cautiously enter everything hits me at one time; the warmth, the sweet fragrance, and your beauty that's one of a kind, as your eloquent body floats atop the steamy water like a dove, with your bright brilliant face shining brightly like an angels sent from above, lighting up the whole room like the celestial light from the sun, while our eyes lock our thought patterns become one. I teasingly undress and begin to walk your way, as your hands come up and wrap around my waist, then they slide up and around my neck, as you pull me forward until our lips connect, with our tongues twirling around back and forth, the flames of desire leave our bodies feeling scorched, while my hand trails from your shoulder down the silky curves of your vivacious breasts, causing your nipples to snap at attention from my gentle caress. Hesitantly I take a step back and peer into your eyes, making sure this is what you really

8

want with this being our first time. What I see in your eyes is you searching, wanting and needing so badly, and I'm sure my eyes reveal that filling those desires is something I'll do gladly. After drying off you escort me to your bed, where your fingers ghost over my face and head, touching my brows, eyelids, and nose; then moving on to learn the texture of my cheekbones. From there tracing over my lips as if trying to memorize the shape, before your lips cover mine as all reserve escapes, with our kiss drumming wildly through our blood like thunder, while our limbs become entangled with one another's, with us only easing up for me to ease it in, which causes the muscles in your thighs to tighten, as your flesh stretches to accommodate my shaft, the once quiet house becomes filled with your moans and gasps. Our lovemaking continues on until we both release, with your body convulsing violently, I explode to the point I can't see, but what matters most is the bond between you and me.

Sincerely yours,

Dinner Invitation

Dear Sunshine,

    You have been invited to dinner for two. Every little thing that goes on tonight must remain between me and you. Wear something nice, but not too nice just in case you get dirty. I plan on skipping the small talk and getting right into flirting. As we sit at the table deciding what will be our appetizer. You suggest starting at your spot would be wiser. So I begin gently kissing all over your spot. All of a sudden the temperature starts to get hot. Slipping off your dress, while your body I caress, then working my way with my tongue to your nipples, sucking on them as they turn as hard as nickels. From there continuing south, covering every inch of your body with my mouth. Just before I reach your clit, you start playing with my dick, pushing it up and down, as your knees hit the ground, starting at the very tip, working your way down till my balls almost touch your lip, sucking on it nice and slow, making my body yearn for mo. Then I tell you to have a seat, as I massage and kiss on your feet, then once again I'm on the move, determined to make it to make it to that groove. As I near it I stop at your tender thighs, and gaze into your deep beautiful eyes, taking only a moment before I continue where I left off, knowing that this time nothing is gonna make me stop. Then I commence to make love to your clit, out of nowhere you sing out "Oh Shit!" Following that I hear a lot of moans as your juices start flowing, your desire and lust for more really starts showing. For a brief second you are overwhelmed and forget how to act, you begin pushing my head from front to back. Then you tell me it's time for the main course, and to hold back nothing with no remorse. As I ease it in, I feel

10

your body tighten, the deeper and deeper I get, the tighter and tighter your grip gets. I slow down for a while, and glance at you to see you smile; looking again into your eyes, wondering how long the heat will rise. I reach over to the fan to make the room colder, then lift your legs over my shoulders, going deeper now I'm really pressing against your walls, with your juices flowing all over my balls. As I go even deeper you don't know whether to feel pleasure or pain. If I'm keeping track right this is the 3rd time you came, then screaming out not only in English but Spanish and French, I thank God there is no terrible stench. Then we get back in the position we started in, as we continue I feel your nails pressing into my skin, your grip getting stronger and stronger, finally I can't hold it any longer. As I let it all go, I feel you let it go too, at that moment I feel as one with you. Then we fall asleep in each other's arms, waking up that way the next day when we hear the alarm. Then getting dressed and going our separate ways, knowing we'll both remember this dinner always.

Sincerely yours,

Dinner Invitation Part 2

Dear Sunshine,

Once again you have been invited to dinner for two. But this time on the menu I have more erotic things to do. I've put together an evening that at the thought of it will have you licking your fingertips, as you tease and please your clit, and massaging your tits, while imagining the orgasmic sensation of my manhood's penetration. Your pussy getting so wet the moisture is saturating your inner thighs, while you pray this isn't a dream when you open your eyes. When you do you see a passionate pair gazing back at your own. Now that you know this is for real you let out a slight moan, that sounds more like the purr of a kitten, as you rub your left nipple that was just bitten, then sucked, then licked with your other hand grabbing a handful of my dick. Laying your sculptured body atop the sheets, as I seductively trace my tongue from your neck to your feet, intentionally leaving out your clit on my first descent down, planning on making love to it on the second go round. Coming back up and easing my tongue in and out of those juicy lips, which hydrates my mouth after that long trip. Now I got your body trembling and tingling all over, as I pull out a surprise that hums like a small lawn mower, inserting the tip of the vibrator into the mouth of your vagina, I begin licking the juices off your clit as if I'm trying to clean fine china. You twitch and shake as the vibration massages your G Spot, feeling the need to grab something you reach out a squeeze my cock. Hearing me moan from the pressure you put on my dick, you lean over and kiss the tip. As I feel your warm moist mouth consume more of me my body becomes weak and my mouth unable to speak.

12

That's when you pull out a surprise of your own, that causes me to moan and groan, with nothing but pleasure, as you handle my balls like a sunken treasure, then squeezing the juices from a mango on my pole, as you press my balls together making a bowl, then tracing the path the juices took with your tongue, making the rest of my body go numb. Then easing my left ball in your mouth and humming a tune, as it vibrates in your mouth I know if I don't stop you I'm gonna cum soon. Grabbing the mango I decide to return the favor, as I begin sucking the juices from your clit which is now mango flavored. Just as you are about to let it go I thrust my tongue in deep as I hear you scream out "Ooooooooo!" in between "Yeessss!" and "Oooooo! Yeesss!" Without giving you a chance to react, I turn you over on your stomach and enter from the back. After your second orgasm I notice tears in your eyes, but your pussy is so hot, juicy, and wet I just can't stop and ask why. Screaming louder than ever I just knew the neighbors would complain, as you cum again I can tell my dick is driving you insane. Your skin tingling toes curling, and back arching. Feeling you are about to cum yet again you take control and put me on my back, whispering in my ear "Daddy I wanna ride you Lac" while holding my dick and spanking the head against your clit, then straddling me placing one leg over each shoulder at a time, causing me to say "Baby you're one of a kind." With my dick deep inside you begin rocking with a melodic groove, our eyes meet each other's and for a brief moment don't move. The moment is broken by your scream, as we both release you churn your ass up and down converting our cum to cream. Feeling weak in the knees you try to balance yourself as you get up so you don't fall, with juices still flowing from your pussy like Niagara Falls. Lying there curled up next to me with your head on my chest, and my arms wrapped snuggly around you like a bulletproof vest. Feeling safe and secure you fall asleep in my arms. Unlike last time we sleep through the alarm. Waking up that day in shock as we look at the clock, until out eyes met, with images of last night making your pussy wet, as my manhood begins to rise we both realize dinner isn't over yet.

Till we meet again…

Sincerely yours,

Letter Of Passion

Dear Sunshine,

I'm gonna call this what it is a sexual invitation, filled with lust and passion that makes this a temptation. One that with you I would gladly give in, as I imagine caressing your golden brown skin, just before I lead you to the bathroom where I have a hot steamy bath waiting, I put on some slow jams to add to this perfect moment in the making. After sensually undressing each other we ease into the tub, once settled in I give your nipple a gentle rub, and then begin washing you from head to toe, going over those special areas nice and slow. Then you take the body wash and begin to return the favor, creating an aroma that's strawberry flavored, with suds all over our bodies we drain the water and turn on the shower, just seeing the water run down those curves is filling me with sexual power. Desire building up to where you can see it in my eyes, so you turn around while I run my hands up and down your thighs, while you arch your back placing your palms against the shower walls, looking over your shoulder to see me standing tall, then shutting your eyes and clenching your teeth as I penetrate your kitty kat, trying not to purr out loud as I hit that, then getting bold using the wall to push your hips back, causing me to go deeper as I go back on the attack. Picking up the pace and intensity now, until I almost slip and fall down, which produces a sigh of relief and a smile on your face, I smile too and suggest a change of pace. So after drying each other off we head to the bedroom, where the only lights shining are scented candles and a cloudless moon. At that moment we kiss and I forget the rest of the world, as I think to myself " I'm fend to give my best to this girl, and romance her until

15

the sun rises, falls, then rises again, and be content with doing that for years on end." My thought are disrupted by something you said, then you gently pull me over to the bed, laying me face down using massage oil to rub my shoulders, working your way down to my lower back then turning me over. As you cover every inch of my body as best as you can, I reach up and palm your breast with my left hand, then use the other to pull you down next to me, now it's my turn to make you feel like you're on ecstasy. With your back to me I begin to give you a full body massage, as I work the right places you whisper "Oh God!" After I finish I reach over and feed you a grape while you suck on my finger and thumb, then you feed me a melon and kiss the juices from my lips with your tongue. As you stroke my manhood it begins to rise, in response I place my fingers in between your thighs, running them over the slivers of your hair, as I take in the aroma of this sex filled air. As your legs spread wider making Miss Kitty completely open, I ease my finger inside your wetness curling it in a come here motion. Your eyes roll back as you whisper my name, with shudders and spasms I can tell you came. As you lay there with your wondrous breasts reaching toward the ceiling, I kiss on one with my fingers soaking in the wetness that's building. Right about now I'd say it could flood the Hoover Dam, looking like a waterfall as I slowly move my hand. Then we turn like cats pleasuring each other at the same time, as you massage me with your tongue I feel a tingle run up my spine. As your mouth consumes more of my growing part you stop savoring and stare, saying "It's hard to believe all this goes in there," I nod as my tongue slithers in and out of your clit, sucking on the meaty part as you bite your lip, your eyes begin to roll as if you're drowning in pleasure, "coos" escaping your lips as play with your treasure. As you release again your body shakes and twitches about, from the vibration I can hear the sound of your orgasm as it feeds into my mouth. I ease my face out and look up to see you smile, and then you tell me to lay back and relax because my tongue just swam a mile. As I lay there your tongue glides from my naval to chest, while your hand settles on my shaft and strokes it with finesse, clamping your mouth down on my neck as my skin grazes your flesh, straddling me now with your thick powerful thighs, hovering over my hips as you ease down half closing your eyes, biting your lip slowly while finding your rhythmic groove, as I lay there stunned by the way you move. I'm almost at my boiling point as I'm being tossed around in your tropical storm, my eyes are on fire as I push myself up on my forearm, at the same time letting out a low intense growl, just before I say "Let me please you now." You look into my eyes and reply, "My pleasure is your pleasure, and you best believe I'm down for whateva." Then you push me back flat as you continue your seductive dance, I was plotting on flipping the script but never got the chance. I practically sit up as I finally release, reaching out and grabbing a handful of cheeks; my eyes roll back as the world disappears, until I hear your ever so sweet voice in my ear. Both of us exhausted every trace of energy gone, as we lay there cuddled up so close as if we are one, symbolically sharing one heart and one mind, as we wonder whether or not our destiny is intertwined.

Sincerely yours,

Sex On A Beach

Dear Sunshine,

I'm about to set the stage for our next rendezvous, picture a private beach with just me and you, as we walk hand in hand from the beach house to the shoreline, practically gliding over the sand whose texture can only be defined as smooth and fine, with no hidden surprises awaiting underneath as we take each step, nearing the water we pause to take in the beautiful sunset, with colors ranging from orange to red to pink, just taking in this moment with you has me afraid to blink, at least until I glance at you and catch your seductive wink, immediately followed by you biting your lower lip, already knowing what time it is I pull you in close by your hips, nibbling on your ear and kissing on your neck, while my fingers slide your thong to the side to play with Miss Kitty who is now wet. After massaging your wetness for a few brief moments you turn to where we are face to face, then you kiss me passionately before you tell me we have to move to another place. A look of puzzlement begins to appear, as I wonder what's wrong with getting down to business here. You assure me that good things happen to those wait, then reach down and grab a handful as you escort me to the next part of our date. At first I reluctantly agree, until it dawns on me that you have something up your sleeve. After a few yards you inform me we're almost there but you want it to be a total surprise. You then remove my shirt and turn it into a blindfold as you cover my eyes. Now you really got me wondering what all you got in store, all this built up anticipation is making me lust for you more and more. After what seems like a decade you tell me we have finally arrived, then directing me to a

18

blanket you carefully lay me on my side, then slowly roll me on my back, just when I'm about to remove the blindfold you sing out "Don't even think about touching that!" Before I can even protest I feel a pair of cuffs clamp down on both wrists, followed by you whispering "Just trust me" in my ear then giving me a quick kiss. At that moment I decide to play along, but in the back of my mind I'm hoping you won't keep me waiting too long. As I lay there submissively allowing you to take control of tonight's events, I hear a lighter strike and smell the fresh aroma from the candles scent. Just as I was beginning to enjoy the sweet fragrance of the candles and the sound of the crashing waves, you quickly wake me up from my daze, with chocolate syrup poured on my chest, followed by whip cream which you also apply to your breast, allowing me a quick taste before you go back and finish what you started, as your tongue begins to trace over the syrup my dick begins to harden. As it glides over my abs I feel my shorts being removed, with two squirts of syrup running down my shaft, you follow it tongue first until the tip makes you gasp. Coming up slowly and taking a deep breath, before you deep throat me again sucking on the shaft until no syrup is left. While this is going on words in my mind just cease to exist, all I can do is lay there motionless, with my mouth wide open and my hands balled in a fist, knowing you have me on the ropes you decide to ease up a bit, with a sigh of relief I say "Oh Shit," little did I know it is far from over yet, before I can even lick my lips you saddle up and insert me into something wet. Just as I was bracing myself for the ride of my life, you whisper in my ear "It aint even going down like that tonight." If it wasn't for the blindfold you would probably end up seeing a grown man cry, well that was before you told me the reason why. In your most sexy seductive voice you say to me, "I wanna

19

taste you and me at the same time when you cum Daddy."
After getting yours right quick and cumin all over my dick,
you keep your end of the bargain. This time until the job is
done there aint gonna be no stopping. It only takes a little
while to catch your rhythm and once again have me on the
verge, with the way you are licking, sucking, and stroking
my manhood its only a matter of time before I give into that
urge. With your body on page with mine you already know
what is about to be. As a reward for being so cooperative
you remove the blindfold to let me see. Truth be told I'm
only able to make out what's going on briefly until my
vision blurs and is gone. My eyes stay rolled back in my
head until the explosion is done, following a few after
shakes the cuffs are removed as I begin to regain sight. One
of the first things I notice is the once beautiful sunset has
transformed into a full moon engulfed by the night. Then I
feel your head on my chest with soft breaths in tune with
mine, as flashbacks of what just transpired run through my
mind. I smile and think to myself "How can I return the
favor," as I look around and notice some of the other goodies
you've staged I realize tonight is definitely gonna be a night
to be savored.

To be continued…

Sincerely yours,

Sex On A Beach Part 2

Dear Sunshine,

As I attempt to recreate the scene in my mind where I last left off, I'm reminded of how your skin felt so smooth and soft, as my hand glides gently over familiar terrain, taking in all the points of interest of your vivacious frame, enjoying every minute of having you cuddled up next tome, in the meanwhile formulating a plan to bring you to ecstasy. With that in mind I proceed to set my plan in motion, as I reach for the pair of beads next to the K-Y lotion, then I position you comfortably on your back, before I hand you the blindfold and say "You already know what to do with that." After making sure the blindfold is secure around your eyes, I pause for a moment to build the suspense for this sensual surprise. Then reaching down with questing fingers lightly brushing your nipples until they bloom with desire, followed by my tongue investigating the smooth plumpness of your delicate peaks as they rise even higher. After a very thorough investigation, my tongue heads south as it continues its exploration, slowing just before reaching the area where your wetness marks the spot, I can feel your muscles tighten as if to say "Please don't stop!" I happily oblige as I take your wetness into my mouth, showing you by pure actions that pleasing you is what I'm all about. I can tell by your response I'm licking all the right places, your body language speaking loud and clear as you start making different faces, accompanied by your coos and moans filling the night sky, as you release your back arches upward as if you can fly, while my tongue laps it all up in a cat like manner, you try to express your pleasure in words but struggle with proper grammar, as if you're drowning in this

21

orgasmic sensation, barely forming a sentence you say "Damn mmm… Daddy… how do you get me … Oooooo in these situations!" I eagerly demonstrate by pushing your knees to your shoulders to widen your clit, as I taste the meaty part of your upper lip, and then write soft messages with my tongue on your fleshly folds, that show you I treasure your nectar more than silver or gold. Now I got your juices flowing like a freshly split ripe cantaloupe, leaving your pussy wet enough to seal a thousand envelopes. With your body now primed and ready I again reach for those beads, taking the medium size ones first I insert balls one, two, and three; while my tongue playfully massages your clit, taking your mind off the 6th ball just put in it, then I reach down for the smaller set of beads, I tell you to relax as I insert them into your forbidden hole gently, one at a time until I reach the 8th ball, that's when your muscles really started to tighten as you contract your walls. To help ease the tension I pull one out of each place, catching the excess juices in my mouth as I savor the taste, then I let my tongue travel north to revisit your upper regions, making your breasts shine with my saliva as if they just went through a rainy season, moving onto your neck as I plant soft kisses, nearing your ear I whisper "I want you to see me get down to business." Then I remove the blindfold and gaze into your light hazel eyes, giving them a chance to adjust to the night sky, you pull my face in close and lick your nectar off my lips, then allow your tongue to explore my mouth as we passionately kiss. I end up having to force myself to ease back, after all I'm a man on mission whose turn it is to be on the attack, so I seductively retrace my steps as my tongue snakes down your skin, until it's slithering all around your femininity again. As I commence to losing myself in your Bermuda's triangle, you spread your legs to give me a better angle, which I use to my advantage to make you climax, as I reach for the strings to begin the final act. Without giving you any warning of what's about to go down, I suddenly yank both strings making all the beads hit the ground. The sudden jolt makes your body jerk and shake, if I didn't know any better I'd swear you was going through a major earthquake, with your non stop moans sounding both painful and beautiful at the same time, along with tears of joy flowing down your face in a straight line, not to mention you start seeing shades of bright red and brilliant yellow, and your body has gone limp like a bowl of Jell-O. I try to drink as much as I can from your fountain but have to call it quits, cuz it was like tying to put the whole Pacific Ocean in one bucket, so instead I watch you float slowly from the clouds, with a smile on your face as you near the ground, that suddenly turns into a devilish grin. Uh – Oh … I know that look … it means you're ready to go at it again.

To be continued…

Sincerely yours,

Sex On A Beach Part 3

Dear Sunshine,

   As I think back on all the events that took place tonight, my grin matches yours as my mind relives all the pleasure and delight, from the way your body felt, tasted, and responded to mine; if only I had God's remote I'd press rewind. I aint trippin though because your eyes is a dead giveaway, basically letting me know you're down to create an instant replay, which is all gravy because I'm always down to make a highlight, even though we started at sunset and are still going in the wee hours of twilight, almost a minute passes by before temptation get the best of us. I guess it didn't help that we still have more of your goodies laying next to us, as my mouth covers your breast and my finger tickles your clit, you let your hands run down my abs until they rest on my dick, then you work your magic as you get my manhood to stand erect, in the meanwhile I do my thing and get your pussy soaking wet. With us both on the same page we let our private parts connect, I enter cautiously as if this were the first time we met, then taking long deep strokes as I fill your well, while your already plump nipples begin to swell, now that you caught my rhythm we're really grooving, shifting into 3rd gear now we're really movin, as the heat rises in between your legs, you start taking short breaths as you pant and beg, then I ease more of myself in as I fill your void, followed by a warm liquid sensation now I feel your joy. I slow down a bit to let you recover from your trembles and shakes, while I bask in what feels like the equivalent to the Great Lakes. After a brief moment I pin your knees to your breasts, balancing myself with my arms as I hold your legs in place with my chest. Now I'm hitting

24

place that you didn't even know existed, while you cry out "Damn Daddy you're gifted!" I respond by telling you "You're really God's gift to me." You reply to that by cumin passionately. The muscles in your legs violently rise and fall, leaving you with that look on your face as if you are in total awe. I slowly ease back allowing your legs to touch the ground, as my eyes search for the K-Y warming jelly which appears no where to be found. Just when I was fend to give up and come up with a new plan, I spot it half buried underneath the sand, which puts me in a more relaxed mood, as I go to retrieve the tube, squirting some into the palm of my hand I then apply it to my shaft, wiping the excess jelly over your ass. A puzzled look appears on your face as you wonder what about to transpire, and then putting the pieces together your demeanor reveals desire being set afire. Trusting me with your body you go with the flow, as I situate your legs your legs to how they were moments ago, except this time I enter your forbidden palace, this time looking into your eyes I see a look of malice, as you grit your teeth and press your nails into my skin, your moans and groans are carried off by the gentle wind. After getting the tip in I work my way deeper inch by inch, watching your facial expression mimic that of the Grinch. Now my rhythm is deep and long, as my strokes come down hard and strong, you scream out as you begin to rant and rave, drowning out the sound of the crashing waves. Right about now I see the thin line between pleasure and pain, but I guess it was all worth it by the way that you came, as your juices flow downward providing more lubrication, I increase the intensity of my penetration, causing you to wail out like a banshee, while your nails dig in as you clamp me, making me experience some of that pleasure and pain, but I aint fend to let up especially with you screaming my name, which

25

does nothing but boost my ego as I pick up the pace, with a burning desire to meet you at the finish line at the end of the race, finally coming around the curve and hitting the last stretch, I pull out and explode all over your chest, losing control like all my motor skills are gone, as my body twitches as if I got Turrets Syndrome. When I finally recover I collapse by your side, with both of us out of breath as we float down from cloud 9. As we lay there gazing upward into the sky, watching the majestic transition of the sunrise, as its brilliant rays highlight the features of the sea, your radiant beauty highlights all your attractive qualities. With the cool breeze blowing in off the ocean, we lay there cuddled up with only our thoughts in motion.

Sincerely yours,

Pleasure Cruise

Dear Sunshine,

Even as my pen touches down on this pad, thoughts
of you begin to surface that I didn't even know I had,
creating a sweet melody that reaches the depths of my soul,
bringing to life fantasies about you that until now have
remained untold. As I try to put them in order by the way
they come to mind, I decide to pick up where I last left off
describing our sensual vacation time. And what a time that
was I can still feel the passion from the sex on a beach,
which at just the brief thought of it produces dimples in your
cheeks. And from the glossed over look on your face I can
tell you feel the same way. Probably wondering just like I
am what's about to go down today. As we leave the private
beach and hit the open road, we take one final look back
before we turn that chapter closed. The short drive to the
docks is made in silence, as we take in our surroundings full
of both beauty and vibrance. Reaching the cruise ship about
an hour before it is time to set sail, we stow away our
luggage and stand by the ships rail, with your bottom
snuggled up to my groin and my fingers intertwined with
yours at your thighs, we enjoy the cool breeze and peer into
the pure blue water that reflects the clear blue skies.
Standing there in a trance like manner until the ships sudden
movement almost made us lose our balance. After laughing
it off you ask me "Are you up for a challenge." I reply, "Its
whateva I'm always down to do damage." And just like that
I'm overcome by a ravenous hunger; until you flip my
emergency brake by saying "You have to wait a lil longer."
Before I can even ask why you give me the look that says it
all, then to clarify what it meant you whisper softly in my

27

ear "Meet me hear at night fall." Then you plant a soft kiss on my firm jaw line and sashay away, leaving me vexed as I watch your voluptuous hips sway. Once you are out of sight I go to the bar to kill time, in the mood for something different then Hennessey I order Tequila with a lime. Four in a half shots later I realize I'm running late, so I throw back the rest of the shot and stagger off to my date. When I finally arrive I can tell you've been waiting for a while, you ask if I'm drunk and I reply "No!" in denial. Instead of making a big deal out of my obvious lie, you step in close and peer up into my dark brown eyes, as I return your gaze my drunken state loses its appeal, thinking clearly now I meet your advances until our lips make a seal. When they finally part my tongue probes your mouth until our tongues met, making our kiss hot, turbulent, and wet, tearing at your robe to expose your breasts, I realize that's all you're wearing as I growl "Oh Yeesss!" then letting the tips of my fingers stroke your under curve, as you let out a sigh indicating I touched a nerve, while your hands are clutched at my head then ease down to examine the texture of my earlobes, in the meanwhile I've almost set your body free from your velvet robe, as you let your curious hands trail down my jaw line to my chest, encountering the springy jungle as your hand gentle begins to massage it with finesse, in response the hand on your breast becomes more possessive and arrogant, while the other hand plays in your wetness as you begin sporadic pants. As I softly kiss on your neck I comment on how you taste sweeter than a honey suckle, while your hands trace down my abs and undo my belt buckle. Once my clothes finally join your robe in a heap on the ground, my desire takes over as I spin you around, then bend you over the rail and tell you to hold on for dear life, as I penetrate you from behind you scream out into the night, while I take

28

a few strokes to catch my rhythm because of the shifting ocean, as my deep thrusts become one pounding motion. Now you're screaming in pleasure at the top of your lungs, as you release the liquid sensation starts to run, which makes me want to join you in that heavenly bliss, so I do as I come with one final stroke and a seizure as I twitch. After we recoup we dress and head back to our suite. I ask about round two but exhaustedly you say we need our sleep. When I inquire why, you look at me, smile, and say "Because tomorrow you're gonna need your strength." With that said you roll over and commence to dreaming, I eventually follow suit as I drift off pondering what you are scheming.

Until tomorrow…

Sincerely yours,

Pleasure Cruise Part 2

Dear Sunshine,

      I must admit the sleep did do me good, too bad I can't say the same for when I sat up and stood. Maybe I did have one two many drinks, as disoriented as I feel my mind is definitely the weakest link, so I sit back down until the migraine left. That's when I notice a note on the stationary desk. After slowly reaching for it I glance over what it has to say, then reread it for a 3rd time as I shake my head in dismay. The whole note is an itinerary of what all you want to do today. Beginning with breakfast at the ships outdoor restaurant, with a warning written in bold letters to be there at **8:30 SHARP!** Judging by the clock I have about 20 minutes to get ready and 3 to get there on time, I end up cutting my shower 5 min short in case I run into a long line. The last thing I want is to be late for the second time on a row. It's a good thing I did because folks are lined up for miles as if they are giving away free tickets to the Oprah Winfrey Show. After a pretty decent meal we move onto the next event, which consists of an aerobic work out that leaves me spent. Moving on to the third thing on our agenda that makes me sigh "Oh God," along with coos and moans as we enjoy the afternoon at the spa. Following that we retreat back to our room and relax in the Jacuzzi, while we debate on whether or not to go to the ships theater to catch a movie. I don't know if it is just the hot steamy water or the fact that we're both in the nude, whatever the case your itinerary just went down the tube, as my hand glides up your narrow ribs to lightly cup your breasts, your eyes become smoky with desire as I stroke your nipples with finesse, then I lean in close and let my lips plant kisses starting at your hairline and

30

trailing down the side of your face, making sure I go over your tenderest spots with precision and grace, as you moan with longing you arch closer and wrap your arms around my neck, pulling my lips closer to yours as they passionately connect, as our tongues explore each others mouth the rest of the world disappears in my head, when it finally reappears I notice our kiss has taken us to our bed, where my hand follows the womanly curve of your hip, while you softly display affection to my neck with your lips, as my thumb draws slow repetitive circles on your coral peaks, which captivates your senses as you struggle to speak, while your nipple forms a hard bud awakened by passion and desire, as I greedily take your bud into my mouth an exploding sensation rises in your chest setting your breasts afire. I pause briefly enough to whisper in your ear, "Baby you taste the way you appear," you reply "Daddy tell me more about the flavor of my skin." I answer back "Baskin Robbins couldn't even capture your flavor that's ever so warm, sweet, and golden." From there my tongue traces down to the dimple of your naval as it dances to an erotic tune, from the way your breathing becomes ragged I can tell you're feigning to come soon. Wanting to taste your sweet juices I hold back your thighs pulling you into my mouth, as you scream with delight as your juices begin pouring out. After getting my fill it is time for my senses to take that ride, so with your thighs still held back I position myself over your hollow and ease inside. That's where the good cop retires and the bad cop takes over, to get more leverage I push your thighs down even lower, then skipping 2nd and 3rd gear I kick it into overdrive, like a wild animal that's been overly deprived, in response you begin to cry out and claw the bed, as I go deeper inside you begin to bite the pillow and clutch the spread, each breath you take becoming more heavy and

31

thick, as your walls stretch from the rowdy thrusts of my dick, that causes a rampaging orgasm that almost throws me back, as your body jerks and your muscles contract, now I'm like a bull that has just seen red, as I pick up where I left off with full steam ahead, your three letter moans turn into 4 letter words, then as you chant my name I give into that surge. As I erupt my mind drifts from this place, as it revels in pleasure spinning out in space. Finally after an unknown amount of time I float back down to earth. Feeling like a new man that's gone through the process of rebirth. Lying down next to my partner in crime, as we ponder how to break the laws of traditional sex one law at a time.

Bo voyage

Sincerely yours,

Winter Paradise

Dear Sunshine,

As the ship continues its course of its West Coast tour, we stop in at British Columbia just long enough to learn how to pronounce bonjour, then we're off again traveling the high seas, heading northwestward where the temperature changes from warm to icy. Finally after a long days worth of travel we dock at one of Alaska's secluded ports, and are driven in snow mobiles to a private resort, that's the size of a small town, with individual electric powered log cabins scattered all around. After finding our unit that's fittingly marked "Unit 69," I'd have to say that we both undressed in record time. If getting bucky naked was an Olympic relay, you'd see us taking home the gold every time on the replay. Going at it now like wild animals trying to out savage the other, as we thrash about the bed getting half tangled in the covers. We slow down just long enough to set ourselves free, then our mouths open up to each others greedily, in the meanwhile our hands flirt with each others erogenous zones, until you assist in guiding me home. Immediately upon entry I begin to establish my domain, as my dick coaxes your deep spots you quiver with excitement as you came. After you recover you express your desire to be on top, in a sweet voice you say "Daddy I wanna ride you until you pop." Then easing down seductively on my dick, as my manhood grazes your clit, you bite your bottom lip, as your femininity opens up to my tip. While your wetness lubricates the path so I can slide deep inside, your gyrating hips bounce up and down and roll side to side, making my eyes close in agony from this sensual pleasure, as my hands that were cupping your ass now apply pressure. When my eyes do open I quickly become hypnotized by the way your nipples are bouncing around, enjoying being in control you demand "Who's running things now!" Me not being in a position to argue I reply, "You are baby…" followed by "Damn your fire ass pussy is driving me crazy." In response you say "Daddy you aint seen nothing yet," which you prove by what you do next. While my shaft is still buried inside your pleasure spot, you ease up a bit and do a 180' like a traffic cop. Words can't even describe the way you are backin' it up. Luke would have a heart attack if he could see the way your ass is actin' up. With one hand on your backside and the other slapping your cheeks, as I watch the ripple effect that appears to go on for weeks. While one of your hands massages my balls with finesse, your walls seem to soften as my manhood is being caressed. As my leg wobbles I take one final look at my Captain at the helm, before my back starts to spasm as I'm catapulted into another realm. When I finally come to I feel your arm draped over my chest, as you lay beside me peacefully getting some well deserved rest, my mind begins to daydream about all the things we haven't tried yet.

To be continued…

Sincerely yours,

Winter Paradise Part 2

Dear Sunshine,

I'm going to do a little fast forwarding in the narrative
of our Winter Solstice, on day to we skied and ice-skated
now on day three we decide to explore a bit. After loading
up on everything we could think of, we set our sights on the
mountain towering above. To an experienced climber it
wasn't all that high, but with us being beginners the
mountain seems to touch the sky. We quickly proceed before
either one of us tries to back out, beginning the ascent we
follow the markers showing us the easiest route, at least I
hope it is because its way too late to turn around. The last
thing you want to do when going up is look down. As we
half climb and half walk the trail that leads to the top, we
notice the temperature suddenly drops, followed by arctic
chilling winds, which begin to crystallize the stubble on my
chin. I look over at you to make sure you're ok, seeing the
concern in my eyes you give me the thumbs as we continue
on our way. As we progress the wind suddenly ceases but
only for a while, then picking right back up bringing with it
another trial. At first the moist snow comes down in a sparse
spray, then turning into a flurry as it covers the markers
guiding our way. Standing there at least 700 ft high in total
confusion, we decide to seek shelter from the blizzardly
intrusion. As we wander around I find myself numbly
drifting in and out of a daze, until I hear you sing out "Look
there's a cave!" Excitedly we slush through the snow
towards the shelter, nearing the entrance we sigh with relief
as we escape the subzero weather. Entering the cave we gasp
with amazement as we turn on the flashlights, the opening is
filled with jagged icicle stalactites and stalagmites. As we

35

light up the interior we are mesmerized by the forest of wild and beautiful ice formations, highlighted by a sky of ice crystals glittering in imitation. Upon reaching the back of the cave we decide to build and cuddle up next to a fire, as we bask in each other's warmth we become filled with desire. That fiery chemistry beginning to ignite, as our lust for each other begins to take flight. With one of your hands around my neck pulling me hard onto your lips, while my left hand traces over the contours of your hips, and to think just moments ago we almost froze, but now with our body heat rising we begin to shed our clothes. As my fingers search your private places you let out a soft moan, while my lips kiss your temple working their way down to your blessed high cheekbone, then I let your ear experience the sweet nuzzlings of my mouth, as I continue softly kissing my way south, until I reach your taut nipples that grow hard as I savor them, skillfully with my tongue I show you how bad I crave for them, you begin to whimper softly then bring my face to yours, our tongues run ramped like two kids on a shopping spree in a toy store, while your flushed nipples rub against my crisp chest hair, my fingers continue their quest down there, as my hands begin to move gently up your soft warm thighs, your legs spread at the touch as I ease my questing fingers inside, tenderly tracing the shape of your vessel like a potter, I'm overwhelmed by how your flesh is so gentle and smooth like a body of water. Pulling my fingers out you put them up to your lips to savor the taste, as you guide my dick over that magical place. As our bodies melt into one the seasons begin to change, going from the icy cold winter to the warm beautiful spring. Words can't describe the passion running through our veins, nor can they capture the millions of sensations as we both came. As the world falls away leaving only us in the vastness of the universe, completing each other like a sweet melody and a mesmeric verse. Then as earth reappears we notice the storm is finally over. After getting dressed we stand at the entrance with my arms wrapped around your shoulders, both of us in awe as we take in the sight, of the setting sun leaving us with flashes of brilliant lights, that is a mixture of flaming rubies, sparkling diamonds, green emeralds, and topaz so dazzling it appears fired by the sun, as we take in the moment together in my heart I'm certain that you are the one.

Sincerely yours,

My Girl

Dear Sunshine,

On day four we find ourselves back on the ship waving our good-byes, to the crystal palace glistening high in the sky, knowing this part of our voyage we'll both hold dear, because in our hearts this Winter Paradise will always be near. As we lose sight of the port with the ship picking up its pace as it glides over the sea, we decide to hit the bar up and check out the karaoke. Three to four drinks later after sitting through a few humorous and horrible acts, I decide to try my luck with an old school tract. As I go through the list I look over at you to see you glowing with anticipation, bringing the perfect song to mind as I select "My Girl" by the temptations. Now I never could sing but right now to me I sound like a mix between Luther and Percy Sledge, building up confidence I start walking toward the stages edge. As I point in your direction all eyes seem to follow, feeling all the stares you pick up your drink and take a nervous swallow, as I beckon you to join me I can sense you want to put a fight, at least until the DJ puts you on blast with the spot light. After downing the rest of your drink you gracefully walk towards the stage, with the spotlight following your every step highlighting your angelic face. Nearing the stage you take my hand as I guide you up the stairs, while I sing my heart out as if you and I are the only ones there. As the melody fades we find ourselves holding each other tight, with sweet thoughts of doing this every night for the rest of our lives, until out of no where that bar breaks out in an up roaring applause, with the sudden thunderous clapping and whistling catching us off guard, we take a quick bow and try to hurriedly leave the stage, but the

38

DJ calls us back talking about we just won 1st place. After
accepting the award we steal off to our room, where we play
our complimentary copy of that "My Girl" tune, recreating
the moment as we hold each other as tight as we can, to the
point where even the rhythm of your heartbeat I understand,
then releasing slightly as I feel my own heart skip a beat,
while our eyes lock my fingers run through your honey
blond streaks, working my way down to your slender neck,
where I pull you in close and give your cheek a peck, before
I study your body that is sculpted like a work of art but
better, hungrily I lean in until our lips press together, as our
lips part my tongue plunges deep into your soft recess, while
the music in the background changes to one of those songs
by Keith Sweat. Curious hands begin to toy with the top
button on my shirt, as I assist you in removing your skirt,
then with one hand around your waist my other flirts with
the satin strap of your bra, once your breasts are released
from their cage I gaze at them with reverence and awe,
before I begin to suck on your firm but soft pillows, that
makes you sway with delight like a weeping willow, as the
sweet nibbling of my teeth graze your nipples your legs
begin to buckle, causing you to fall back on the bed letting
out a slight chuckle, within seconds I join you as my tongue
traces down the length of your flesh, your breasts rising with
each stuttering breath. After removing your satin thong I
begin to lick around the edges of your clit, struggling to keep
your eyes open you reach down and clutch my head with
your fingertips, as I continue to praise your femininity with
my tongue, I begin to savor the taste of your cum, basking in
it with your sweet aroma on my face, as you continue to grip
my head and float to another place. Coming down now you
notice my dick waiting to enter, you give it the green light as
you let out a soft whimper, while I begin to fill your void,

39

coos and moans express your joy. Finding my rhythm you begin to chant about how much you want me and need me, while your vision blurs with flickering stars as you soar with the wings of a freed being, followed by spasms as you experience a muscle contraction, with every cell in your body fully aware of the ecstatic reaction, right then I come to the point where I can't hold it any longer, as I sprout wings of my own and soar the wild blue yonder. How long the flight lasted I have no clue, all I know is when I land I drift off to sweet thoughts of you.

Sincerely yours,

A Night Of Fireworks

Dear Sunshine,

    Once again I'm awe struck thinking about the time we've shared, with the future looking very promising as we walk hand in hand through the fair. It's been about a month in a half since we came back from our cruise, as my mind takes a trip down memory lane my ears are filled with Jazz and Blues, which brings me back to the present as we stroll through the fair grounds, taking in all the sights and sounds. People everywhere filled with laughs and smiles, from the oldest war veteran to the smallest child. Even the weather is participating in this joyous atmosphere, although the sun's going down the sky is still nice and clear. Nearing the ticket booth we wait our turn then purchase bracelets to ride all the rides, after all we might as well enjoy ourselves to the fullest on this festive night. We decide to start off small and work our way to the bigger ones; so far out of the first four rides the teacups have been the most fun. Two rides later we decide to take a break, mainly because I have an undeniable craving for a funnel cake. After splitting it and downing a couple drinks, we cut in line at the roller coaster by ducking under the chain links, to the dismay of all the other folks waiting in line, but it didn't phase us because we have so much to do and so little time. Boarding the coaster we slowly begin our ascent to the top, upon finally reaching the summit we notice the awaiting 250 ft drop, with impossible loops and sharp curves, as we travel at insane speeds I feel adrenaline flowing through all my nerves. As the ride abruptly comes to an end, the only thought running through our minds is *"Lets do it again!"* So we do it two more times before we call it quits, from the looks we were getting from the folks waiting in line I thought it was gonna come down to fists. Not wanting to spoil the great time we're having we move onto something new. With you spotting a basketball game with one of the prizes being a gigantic Scooby Doo. Always up for a challenge I pay the fee and give it shot. The first attempt misses but the second one drops, which causes you to jump up and down while mimicking child's excited voice, as you skip over to the booth and point toward your choice. Then holding Scooby delicately like a antique Persian rug, you turn and thank me with a kiss and a hug. After walking around a bit I tell you I have a special place in mind, but we have to leave now because we're running out of time. Once settled in my car we set out to the unknown destination. Well at least unknown to you because tonight I got this place designated. Coasting through downtown with hardly any traffic in sight, I finally begin to slow down with the police station to our right. Puzzled you ask, "Where on earth are you taking me." I reply, "Just sit back and relax and you'll see." As I make a left into the seven story parking garage, going up ramp after ramp as we pass by deserted cars. Upon reaching the top, we notice it's a completely empty lot, with a view that overlooks the festive city and active river that has a parade of steamboats traveling across its surface, with the Stars and Stripes waving proudly from their masts with purpose. While your attention is on the wonders below, I'm busy setting up for the 4th of July show, with an extra thick quilt and pillows to match, slow jams playing and candles filling the air with the rich scent of lilac. Before joining you I go to the cooler and come back with two glasses of white wine, as we toast to having a happy 4th of July. With fireworks going off into the night sky, we lay down on the quilt and watch them soar by, and then explode into millions of colors and shades, taking in the moment as if we have gone from adults to kids in the 4th grade…

Sincerely yours,

A Weekend At The Keys

Dear Sunshine,

Baby as the seasons change all round, my love for
you remains true and sound, as I reminisce about the time
we've shared, breathing in your love like a fresh breath of
air, although this is the first time I've openly expressed that
four letter word, our most intimate moments declare it to
where it was clearly heard, and understood without ever
being spoken, creating a bond meant never to be broken.
Going on 3 years together and we still holding on strong,
destiny in the making as we prove we belong. Now that
that's taken care of I'm going to describe our next outing, as
we drive around town the sun is shining brightly with
minimal clouding, I'm reminded of our brief stay at that
private beach. Instead of feeling like several months ago it
feels like only a couple weeks. Drifting back to the present I
note the difference in the atmosphere, with Key West
containing far more beauty along with tourists here. Finally
we reach the Hilton where we'll be staying over the course
of the weekend. Just from the touch of the plush bed I could
be really tempted to sleep in. After getting settled in we set
out on a journey to find something to eat, as we stroll the
boardwalk my ears pick up the drums of a Caribbean beat.
Practically following the tune we find ourselves being led to
its source, as we near the restaurant the aroma drags us in at
full force. As the hostess shows us to the booth the band
plays on, with no vocals just the melody of a tropical song.
After finishing our meal we continue our stroll along the
boardwalk, stopping every now and then to check out some
of the local shops. As the sun starts falling and the moon
begins to appear, we find ourselves taking in the scene at the

pier, before we hit up a random nightclub, after about 30 minutes you say, "I'll be right back I need to freshen up." While you're gone I start to pick up on a strange vibe, then out of nowhere I get hit on by a guy. If it wasn't for you intervening aint no telling how the scene would have played out, with the neck of a bottle clutched in my hand he was fend to be laid out. Once things settle down we leave in search of a straight bar, passing by jugglers, mimes, and musicians as we ride in a streetcar. Taking in the scenery until we reach Bahamas St, then walking the rest of the way to a club called "The Key." Upon entry I quickly scan the crowd to prevent another incident, the last thing I need is for another guy to tell me he'd be willing to pay my rent. With the assessment done I relax as I fetch us a couple drinks, relieved as hell that it's only females giving me inviting winks. Already taken I focus on the task at hand, returning now to our table I pause at the sight of you being courted by some man. A little intrigued by the situation I sit back and watch your reaction, while you appear to be amused by his attempt before you send him packin'. Taking that as my cue I return with our drinks, then we toast to being hit on by men as our glasses clink. Laughing it off I ask did he come up with a good line, you say it was ok but couldn't be compared to mine, at that we toast again and commence to having a good time. After a refill we hit the dance floor, bumpin' and grindin' as if our bodies are at war, with the DJ on point with his mix of club hits, then gradually slowing it down with slow jams and classics. As the party winds down we answer the last call for alcohol, then sip our drinks while I call a cab in a booth against the wall. When we finally reach our room I let you shower first, midway through it thinking to myself I should have joined you as I silently curse. About 10 minutes after the water shuts off you exit the bathroom, smacking me

45

on my bare ass then telling me to hurry back soon. After I finish showering and drying off I open the door expecting a treat, instead I see a note saying to meet you at the pool but to make sure I'm discreet. As I get dressed thoughts of you flash through my mind as I determine that you're truly unique.

To be continued…

Sincerely yours,

A Weekend At The Keys Part 2

Dear Sunshine,

As I maneuver through the lobby slipping out the back exit all cool, I approach my next obstacle being the iron gate around the pool. After clearing the gate I see your silhouette swimming the length of the pool underwater, making sure the coast is clear I strip down and stand by the edge of the water. Coming up for air and leaning your head against the mosaic tiles just above the waterline, drawing in deep breaths as your eyes examine me then meet mine. I then dive off the deep end and torpedo underwater until I slowly surface inches from your face, my arms come up on either side of you pinning you in place, my legs drift closer as my thighs rub up against yours, as I kiss you using my tongue as an instrument of pleasure, your hands coming up examining my face as they trace over the arch of my sleek black brows, then over the bridge of my nose and the sensual curve of my mouth. My lips open catching a daring finger as they stroke down its length, sliding between the base of it and the next one as my tongue shows off its grace and strength. Then my hands find your breasts as they swiftly and carefully remove your bikini top, your nipples becoming firm and erect begging my caressing fingers not to stop. As I continue to reward them for their ready response my mouth slants over your lips, while my other hand slides beneath the bottom of your bikini and eases it down over your hips. With the slow graceful movements of your legs between mine it floats free, as our tongues continue to play tag passionately, I clasp your nakedness to mine with desire kept at bay for a moment as we delight in each others feel only, until your hand seeks out my manhood which was starting to feel lonely. With desire about to erupt I release you and hoist myself over the pools edge, then extend my hand as I help lift you out of the water and over the ledge, our bodies dripping water as I lead you into the darkened cabana, with fulfilling absolute lust being what our bodies are in demand of. I manage to find a large sheet and spread it quickly on the white lounge in the cool dark room, then you sit back on the lounge taking my hand and pulling me toward you, with moonlight your only garment as my mouth opens over your skin, as my tongue laps over your nipple again and again, then hovering over your naval and diving into it with my tongue finding a few drops of water there, looking up I smile and say "Chlorine never tasted so good" as my fingers thread through your damp hair. Softly laughing as you half close your eyes, suddenly the laughter becomes short halting breaths as my kisses continue across your belly to your thighs, then coming up to kiss you while my finger appreciate your spot, with our tongues whirling around making our kiss urgent and hot. As my tongue continues to probe your lips close around it sucking gently with satisfaction, as my body sinks into yours perfectly I shutter with gratis faction. As our bodies dance to the same tune your arms hug me tight with your thighs closing against mine, a wellspring building up and boiling over inside, until its rushing currents engulf you as you clutch me tightly, we plunge beneath the surface together then your grip loosens up slightly. Long minutes later still lying there interlocked breathing deeply of the same air. If it wasn't for dawn approaching I'd be content with staying there. Rounding up our clothing and getting dressed then slipping over the gate, minutes later as my head hits the pillow I begin thinking about tomorrow and suddenly can't wait.

Until then...

Sincerely yours,

A Weekend At The Keys Part 3

Dear Sunshine,

As the sun awakens us from the few hours of sleep we had, instead of feeling tired I feel as energetic as a young lad, who stayed up as long as possible for Santa on Christmas Eve, then waking up early the next day ready to open the presents under the tree, except in my case your lingerie is my wrapping, after removing your bra my tongue waters both of your saplings, causing them to sprout up like pine trees, as our lips meet each others wildly, then slowing briefly to savor each others taste, while we merge into one and quicken the pace. After spending the morning messing up the bed, we finally begin to prepare for the long day ahead, with another one of your itineraries for places to go and things to do. What matters most to me is that I'm spending time with you. The first place we check out is the Lost Treasures Shipwreck Historeum, followed by a fascinating stroll through the Key West Aquarium, then its on to the pier as we prepare for a little scuba diving, just snorkeling over the clear water you're able to see the coral reefs that are lively. As we submerge deeper we can see the current moving the sea grass like the wind blows fields of wheat, as if they are hooked together in one motion nodding to the same beat, with colorful schools of fish traveling in close knit groups, as clown fish swim through obstacles as if they are jumping through hoops. Then you got eels creepin' around rocks and lobsters chillin' at the bottom, as the manna ray swims alone as if everyone is afraid to bother him. Everything was almost perfect as we watch sea horses galloping all around as if they're on a track, until I accidentally lean against a sea urchin as its sharp spikes

49

pierce my ass. From my panicked motions and muffled screams you would have thought I was being attacked by a shark, as I finally break the surface I can already tell it left a mark. No longer wanting to be near the water I decline on going Marlin fishing, as the mark turns into an inflamed knot an ice pack on my ass is what I'm wishing. Of course with me being the type of guy I am I won't vocalize that last request; instead doing some more sight seeing is what I suggest. As we tour the island on this warm beautiful day, we pay our respects to the home of the great Ernest Hemingway. Our next destination was the Dry Tortugas National Park, then it was on to the Sunset Celebration as the sky begins to turn dark, with the fire seeming to die down in the sun making it just a glowing red ball in the sky, as the island is split between a cascading sun and the oncoming night, ranging in colors from orange, pink, and red to purple, navy, and black; while this is going on all life on the island seems to pause for this mystifying act. With our bodies nestled up close we take in the stunning view, until my eyes take notice of you, with yours meeting mine just before we strengthen our embrace, as our lips connect and eyes close our world transforms into an even more magical place...

What a night to be loved

Sincerely yours,

City Of Magic

Dear Sunshine,

　　Baby as I reminisce about the sparkle in your eyes, that could light up the night skies, along with a smile that could brighten up the sunniest of days, bringing more warmth than the hottest of rays. I guess that's why the name Sunshine fits you well, with thoughts of you having the effect of bringing heaven into hell. As we travel through Jacksonville on I-295, we get pulled over for being black while in a nice ride, by a red neck cop who insists on calling me "boy." Claiming I fit the description but I know it's just a ploy, for getting me out of the car to perform frisk search. Mayne if he don't chill I swear he gon get hurt. Luckily he gets a call over his radio, so grudgingly he hands back my license and turns to go, and not a moment too soon as I wait for him to leave before I pull off, then play my Oldies but Goldies CD to help me cool off. As I continue to fume you place your hand over mine and tell me it's gonna be ok, and to look at the bright side we're fend to spend some QT today. With my mind now focusing on what we got planned, my grip on the steering wheel loosens as I relax my hand, with the built up anger beginning to dissipate, as we continue to ride on the interstate, switching to I-10 then to I-75, while singing along with Aretha Franklin's "I Will Survive," with endless rows of trees flying by, and the occasional house off to the side, we travel that route until we merge west on I-20, with the baby blue sky appearing clear and sunny. Finally reaching 6 Flags we prepare to seize the day, by taking on any roller coaster they can throw our way. Then we hit up the Lennox Square Mall to shop amongst the stars, followed by dinning at Gladdis & CeCe's Chicken &

Waffles before walking it off at Centennial Park. From there we follow MLK Dr through the downtown area, passing colleges and the Georgia Dome's colossal exterior, while navigating past sky scrappers that reach towards the heavens, I glance at the clock to see it's half past seven. As we roll up to the infamous Magic City. I catch a glimpse of an old school Cutlass sittin' pretty, as I try to find a space in the back parking lot, then get out and stand in the long line wrapped halfway around the spot. With this being a Tuesday night the place aint crowded with stars, which is a good cuz we avoid paying an outrageous cover charge. The first thing I notice upon entry are two gold poles on the horse shoe shaped bar, then behind that a red curtain shielding the VIP section with ghetto secret service type guards. Connected to the front of the bar is a runway that leads to the main stage, which branches off into two wings that each has golden poles on display. Suspended high above the runway is the DJ booth, with windows surrounding it so that the whole club is in full view. The interior has a red and black color scheme, with matching velvet couches, disco lights, and smoke machines. As the "Whisper Song " by the Ying Yang Twins fade out, "Whistle While You Twerk" energetically bangs out, as wave after wave of strippers come out to do their thing, one in particular intrigues you with her routine. As you look on with peaked interest in your eyes, taking note of the way her curvaceous hips vibrate from side to side, with nice firm breasts covered only by her caramel complexion, and a face that could ace America's Top Model inspection, with features revealing she's a mix between half black and half Asian. Yea I gotta admit Shawty carry a lot of persuasion. While the DJ plays "Freak Hoes" by master P, I give he a 50 spot with instructions to meet us in the VIP. After paying the entry fee we're admitted into the VIP lounge, where there are plush couches and mirrors all around. Wanting a little privacy we pick a couch in the corner, as we sip on our drinks waiting for her to join us. About 5 minutes later the curtains part for her to enter, as she practically glides toward us as if heaven sent her, with all her movements appearing choreographed, from the slight bounce of her breasts to the sway of her ass. Once in earshot she says, "Hi, my name is China Doll, but you can call me China for short it's up to ya'll." With the intros complete she asks what can she do for us tonight. Half jokingly I reply, "I want you to turn out my future wife." In the meanwhile the DJ slows things down a bit with Avant's "Read Your Mind," as China seductively straddles your hips and begins to grind. At first you seem uncomfortably nervous but then begin to relax, as you gradually get into it your hands ghost over her breasts and ass. While this is going on I can see your sensuality wanting to wreak havoc like El Ni o, as the song fades and is replaced with "Slow Down" by Bobby Valentino. Eventually that song fades as well, followed by Master P's "I Can Tell." Reluctantly she informs us that our time is up, and that she wishes our relationship the best of luck. As China is about to turn to go I give her another 50 spot along with my business card, then tell her to call in a week before we head out to the car. Aswe pull off leaving Magic City behind us, something inside tells me that someday the magic will once again find us.

Sincerely yours,

Perfect Storm

Dear Sunshine,

As my thoughts run ramped battling to pass the test, until one victor stands out among the rest, which should have been a no brainer choice for me, after all you're my inspiration and the voice for me. So as I follow your lead and travel back in time, while my ears catch the rhythm of the rhyme, which brings to mind a day that will stay with me forever, that continued even through some stormy weather, but not getting ahead of myself I'm gonna rewind, and pick up from the start with this next line. Once settled in at our hotel we decide to walk the strip, while we discuss trivial things about our trip. Along the way we spot Red Lobster and go inside, and are brought to our table by a wanna be travel guide, who insists on telling us about Virginia Beach, claiming he knew of places that not many people have reached. After taking our order he says he'll be right back, while waiting on our crab legs he suddenly appears with a map. Feeling at liberty he pulls up a chair to explain the scene, more interested then annoyed I let him proceed. When his spill is over I tip him as a sign for him to go, instead he says, "Wait there's just one more thing you should know." I glance your way and catch your approving eyes, then nod in my agreement while I let out a sigh. After listening intently we decide to take his advice, even though it changed our agenda spontaneity is always nice. Upon completing our meal we take our leave, as we step outside we're met by a cool summer breeze, under two puffy layers of silvery gray clouds, giving off the impression that soon the rain will be coming down. But not willing to let anything rain on our parade, we press on in hopes of making it there by midday. First we visit a few local shops until satisfied we bought enough, then briefly stopping by the hotel to drop of most of the stuff. From there we drive down Oceana Blvd, passing the 264 Expressway that's packed with cars. In contrast the road up ahead is clear. *Hmmm… judging by the lighthouse shouldn't the turnoff point be here?* Okay there it is off to my right, slowing down I turn on Shore Dr. After a few miles the beach comes into view, with the vast ocean appearing silvery blue, along with sailboats pasted against the darkening blue horizon, and the sound of sea gulls calling out while gliding. Finally we reach a road called Ocean Mist, and travel it until coming to a dead end flowed by a cliff. Standing there with luminous clouds completely gray, casting its eerie shadow all over the bay. Suddenly it pours down as the wind begins to wail. Hurriedly we grab our gear and head down the steep trail. From there seek shelter in the cove's cave-like inlet, which aint much of a cave but at least its keeping us from getting wet. Too late though with water running in smooth streams over your skin, as my fingertips glide over you arousing dormant places within, our lips lock as our tongues wildly probe, in the meanwhile we begin to shed our clothes. With our limbs entangled the sky suddenly releases a thunderous boom, that shakes even the foundation of this natural made room, followed by lightning bursting into hot white flashes in jagged streaks, as our lovemaking continues until we reach our peaks. Almost in unison the storm lets up and the sky begins to clear, the sun shining brightly with the makings of a rainbow beginning to appear, the ocean smooth and full of promises that it intends to keep, as the gentle wind seems to rock the waves to sleep. Sometimes you never know what changes a storm will bring, but when shared with the one you love it can be a beautiful thing.

Sincerely yours,

New York, New York

Dear Sunshine,

     In the sea of thoughts that begin to flood my mind, I pick out one and focus on that moment in time. As I close my eyes the scene becomes real vivid, causing all of my senses to relive it. Your scent, your feel, and your taste, along with your beauty that my mind just can't erase. Truly this is what fantasies are made of, as we roll through Harlem in my Lac sittin' on dubs, candy mango orange with a white top, along with a complete JL Audio system and air shocks. Most important of all I got you sitting in the passenger seat, looking content as you nod your head to the beat. In the meanwhile we turn off MLK Blvd and onto Central Park West, traveling at a steady pace then taking the 4th left, with the Belvedere Castle and a beautiful lake in full view, then turning down East Dr passing The dairy and a Zoo. Following the loop we exit onto Broadway, while the night sky prepares to invade the day, we pass street after street with buildings standing tall, and billboards announcing the Apollo Theatre and Carnegie Hall. As we reach 7th Ave we stop in at Times Square. Even at this time of day plenty of tourists are there, which is making it difficult to find a decent parking spot. Finally settling for an inconvenient one we begin the long walk. After touring the plaza we enter the NYLA where we have a reservation to dine. Following an exquisite meal we explore the area till around nine, then heading back to the car we drive off into the night, noticing Penn Station off to our right, as we merge onto 6th Ave then turn on 32nd St, we pass a wino wearing nothing but socks over his feet, with torn blue jeans and a worn sweat shirt, and a look in his eyes revealing an unquenchable thirst. In contrast there stands the colossal Empire State Building, appearing to hold up the night sky like a beam holds up a ceiling. Approaching the entrance we find the glass doors locked, with a rent-a-cop shaking his head and pointing to the clock, indicating the building is closed except to authorized personnel, and that all trespassers risk fines or a trip to jail. Acknowledging the warning we walk down the street as we weigh our options. *Lets see ... there's bribery or trying to hit him like Bernard Hopkins.* Naw those won't work I gotta come up with something else, a distraction of sorts involving someone else. *But who can I find at such short notice? Hold up aint that the wino that I first noticed?* Yea that's him I wonder if he's down for the cause, only one way to tell as we wait for the light traffic to pause, then crossing the street I explain to him our situation, then break down our plan for our infiltration. After hearing us out he asks what's in it for him. I tell him to follow me to the Lac and offer a fifth of Gin. At the sight of the bottle his eyes light up like a kids on Christmas day, as he rubs his hands together nodding his head while saying "OK." With the plan finalized we all move into position, as the adrenaline builds up as if this were one of Tom Clancy's tactical missions. Then frantically you sprint up to the door and begin to pound on the glass, with panic in your voice you scream out "Come quick he's having a heart attack!" Alarmed Mr. Top Flight Security bounds for the door, charging towards the wino convulsing in front of the bookstore. Quickly placing your foot in the way of it closing you let out a loud sob, signaling me the coast is clear as the wino continues to do his job. After speedily making our way through the lobby we ride the elevator to the top, with our hearts beating so rapidly it feels like any moment they'll pop. Now tension is building as we wonder how long the guard will be occupied, plus with a camera pointing down at us there's no place to hide. Finally after what seems to be a lifetime we reach the top floor, as the elevator chimes I can breathe easily once more. Just as we step out into the passageway, footsteps echo from not all that far away, that seem to be coming closer and closer with each step. Damn what do we do there isn't much time left? Taking the lead I head off in the direction of the sound, until we're standing face to face with a guard making her rounds. Before she can even question why we're here, I cheerfully greet her then whisper something in her ear. Almost immediately the questioning look gives way to a beaming smile, glancing from you to me she says "This way" and pivots on the polished tile. Practically skipping with delight she leads the way, while chatting about wishing something romantic would happen to her one day. After swiping us through the security gate she points out the observation deck, in return for her understanding kindness I bend down and give her cheek a gentle peck, which causes her to blush shades of red and pink, as she takes her leave she gives you the thumbs up with an approving wink, then half closes the door so that we won't be locked out, with her out of earshot you finally ask "What was that all about?" Innocently I reply "I told her I was gonna propose to you on top of the world, then declare to New York you're my one and only girl." As smiles crease our faces we playfully tour the observation deck, looking for a place to unleash our XXX rated mindset. Finding it our playful manner becomes more aggressive, with absolute lust making our caresses more possessive, as we kiss wildly letting desire take control, our bodies preparing to put on another exhibitionist show, as we ease down to the ground near the guard rail, while my fingers toy with your nipples that have begun to swell. Now lying down

58

with both hands interlaced behind my head, while you pull out my penis and your tongue tickles the head, then lifting your skirt you slide up then back to take me inside, with fingers digging into my shoulders as you catch your stride, in response my hands cup your bottom and begin to knead it gently, as our ragged breaths and moans create a lover's symphony, that seems to magnify and echo everywhere, until a sudden loud gasp slices through the air. Simultaneously we turn our heads in the direction the sound came from, where the female guard contemplates whether to watch or run. I guess her naughty side decided to come out. Speaking into her radio "Alls clear on my route." Then she simply says "Well on with the show," as you without skipping a beat pick up the tempo. Truly this is the essence of adult entertainment, with our spectator watching with aroused amazement, as our bodies violently release like champagne with a popped cork, while our heighten moans declare our pleasure to the city of New York. Mayne, talk about taking a relationship to new heights, and to think this is only one of two very sensual filled nights…

To be continued

Sincerely yours,

New York, New York Part 2

.

Dear Sunshine,

As the excitement in your voice rings loudly in my mind, we make the journey to Upstate New York in record time, traveling the route from the Turnpike to 95 North, as I gun down the pedal for a its worth, along the way noticing the scenery here is like being on a whole new planet, compared to the City where in place of trees buildings are planted, with the sun showing off it daybreak red, but after driving through the night all I can focus on is a warm cozy bed. You on the other hand are soundly asleep, looking comfortable as hell reclined in the passenger seat. Finally reaching our destination we get a room at the Hampton Inn, where I pass out until you awaken me around ten. Groggily I reply, "Go away and leave me alone, " as I roll back over with a slight groan. Refusing to take that for an answer you shake me violently, while in my mind I'm cussin' you out silently. Realizing that until I answer I won't be able to get any rest, I sit up and say, " Whatever the question is the answer is yes." With that said I lay by body back down, and surprisingly I don't hear another sound, but two hours later when I wake up from my peaceful slumber, I notice I'm more alone than a polar bear in Africa in the middle of summer. As I look around the room wondering where you could be. I spot the note you left leaning up against the TV. After reading it twice I shake my head and let out a sigh, because I still have three hours till you return around five. To kill time I order Chinese food and watch the Raiders play the Browns, while you jam to that Ciara track as you drive around town, supposedly from the note you're just out sight seeing, and maybe a lil window shopping but that I aint believing.

Knowing you, you're out on a mini-shopping spree, especially considering your VISA is always where you want it to be. Surprisingly though you come back with only a few bags, claiming there was a sale on essentials that you had to have, with your definition of essentials being clothing by Apple Bottoms and BabyPhat, not to mention a pair of shoes and a purse to match. Wisely changing the subject I ask if you want some of the left over Chinese, but you decline saying "I took myself out to eat." Once settled in we watch an episode of Law and Order, then hop in the Lac traveling toward the Canadian border, with my mind focused on the business at hand, as you explain some of what you got planned. So far it sounds good to me so I'm all for making it happen, while in the background my system bangs out Young Jeezy's story of Trappin. Crossing the border we head for the CN Tower, which has plenty of attractions to keep a tourists busy for hours. Starting in the arcade with air hockey and basketball, followed by a shoot em up game where we capped them all, then hitting up the indoor go-cart track, where we race wildly like a couple of Nascar maniacs. Finally after finishing a few drinks from the restaurant on the top floor, we decide to bounce before we wind up back in the arcade for more. Not knowing our destination I let you drive, while I ride shotgun taking in the clear night sky, with a crescent moon that looks like a prop for a stage play, appearing brilliant enough to out shine the sun on the brightest of days. As I become lost in my thoughts I don't even realize we're back in the U.S. as we listen to that track called "Waterfalls" by Ludacris, which looking back on it was the perfect song for the occasion, as I snap back from my reverent star gazing, to see that we've arrived at Niagara Falls, with its continuous flowing water reflecting the heavens like glowing crystals. Standing at the sidewalk

61

gazing at the rushing river below, with two inward slanted streams causing the rapid current flow. Half hidden between them lies a barely visible platform, with a trail connecting us to it through a veiled mist storm. After cautiously following it we find ourselves taking in the falls from a different point of view, as the clear raging water surrounds me and you, with its spray sprinkling our faces making us feel alive, as our torching kiss conveys all the passion smoldering inside. Practically ripping off our clothing we engage in the art off making love, as the celestial bodies witness it all from above.

Sincerely yours,

Sweet St Louis

Dear Sunshine,

     Just as light pierces through the darkness your love
fills my void, replacing the emptiness with an excitable joy,
that sparks my need to write it all down, as I remember our
trip to the Show Me Town, that all begins with a Mississippi
River boat cruise, where we discover what it was like to live
in Mark Twain's shoes. Next on the agenda is a walk in
Laumerre Park till a light drizzle started, so instead we hit up
the Art Museum and the Botanical Garden. After spending
some time with Mother Nature we say our good-byes, then
head for the Gateway Arch that stands 630 ft high. Finishing
up there we go to the Galleria to check out the upscale
boutiques, until deciding it's time to show you our hotel
suite, where in the bathroom there's a huge garden style tub
sitting on marble floors, enclosed by ceramic walls and a
mahogany door, that leads to the main room with its plush
thick champagne-colored carpet, that sinks down a bit when
you walk across it, with a complimentary bottle of Dom
Perignon' sitting on the black baby grand piano, and a
bouquet of red roses near the floor to ceiling windows, that
provide a beautiful view of the St Louis skyline, and in the
corner a fully stocked wet bar with everything from whiskey
to wine. Upon entry your eyes widen in delight, as you take
in this luxurious sight, turning slowly as you scan the place,
then walking up to the piano and reaching for the vase,
pulling out a single rose, and examining it's beauty before
your eyes close, to take in its freshly cut fragrance, then
turning towards the window and gazing out in utter
amazement, at the sun drifting towards the horizon as if it's
gonna sink, in the tranquil backdrop of dazzling bright pink.
After a few moments you turn back around to discover I'm

gone. In my place lies rose petals to guide you along, as you curiously follow the trail to the bedroom slowly, your ears pick up the sound of R Kelly singing lowly, then your eyes focus on the gigantic bed, with goose feather pillows to rest your head. But what really catches your attention is the gift wrapped box on the gold and black spread, that you savagely attack like a goose going after a piece of bread, revealing one of those sexy lavender teddy things with lace, that you immediately try on in a quickened pace, then model in front of the full length mirror appearing to be content, as I come out of my hiding spot in the walk in closet, wearing nothing but silk boxer briefs, while you watch my hands close over your breasts as soon as I'm in reach, my fingers then arousingly slide down your sides to your waist, then leaning forward I nudge your head backwards until our mouths fall into place, with our kiss igniting desire governed by need and ruled by passion, my hands take the last of your garments with them on their gradual descent over your skin. Then together we look at our images in the mirror before I carry you off to the bed, as we ravish each other like starving beasts of prey waiting to be fed, rolling from one side of the bed to the other, while we lick, suck, and bite one another. Before continuing any further I ask "Are you still open to new things?" You reply "Of course daddy, I'm your queen and you're my king" followed by " together we make an inseparable team, that's why I'm down for whateva knaaimean."

To be continued…

Sincerely yours,

Sweet St Louis Part 2

Dear Sunshine,

Baby these thoughts of mine I just can't suppress, the images of you in my mind simply won't rest. It's like a never ending story that get better with each chapter, made of the stuff men have spent life times seeking after. Once I've set the mood for the rest of our date, I then lead you to the garden style tub that awaits, illuminated by scented candles surrounding it like an alter, with rose petals floating atop the steamy water. Slowly you ease yourself into the tub, once settled in I give your shoulders a gentle scrub, working my way down your back and over your breasts, taking the time to appreciate each one starting from right to left. As the water cools down I assist you out of the tub and dry you off, while enjoying the texture of your skin being so smooth and soft. Then blindfolding you before I guide you back to the bedroom, as you sit down on the bed I say "Baby I'll be back real soon." Practically reading your mind as it wonders where I'm going and why, I answer the unspoken question by saying, "Be patient I have a surprise." With that said I leave but quickly return again, as I bring along a special friend, who immediately sets out on her mission to entertain, while I put on that song "I'm N Luv" (With A Stripper) by T Pain, then post up against the wall watching her do her thing, as she walks over to you wearing nothing but a G string, and removes the blindfold from your eyes, after which you look from her to me in total surprise, until recognition sets from that night at Magic City, with curious desire compelling you to reach out and grab her titty, while China sensually begins her lap dance routine, with her body moving in ways that one could only dream, hips grindin', abs rollin', and breasts dancing to the music, all the while you appear about to lose it, as if all your reserve is on the verge of disappearing, as her lips skim along your cheek to play with your earring, while ya'll slowly recline till you're flat on your back, with her tongue snaking down your body placing all your hot spots under attack, as she drops damp kisses that cool against your warm skin, adding a glossiness that reflects the glow within. When her mouth reaches your breasts you arch your back to draw her in closer, as your body trembles in anticipation of her kisses trailing even lower. While this is going on I'm experiencing a growing anticipation of my own, as my manhood begins to harden like stone, but patience is something that I'm determined to exercise, as I continue to look on with lust welled up in my eyes. With your senses on heightened alert she makes her descent, as she trails downward her nostrils are filled with your fragrant scent, while she spreads your lips open with both thumbs, and learns the texture of your soft flesh with her tongue, as sensations pulse throughout your body that you can't understand, causing you to give into the tidal wave of desire's demand, as you release the mindless current sweeps over your body, while I smile to myself taking that as my cue to join the party...

To be continued

Sincerely yours,

Sweet St Louis Part 3

Dear Sunshine,

As your face glows with complete satisfaction, I begin my approach to get in on the action. Reaching the side of the bed my mouth covers your exposed breasts, devouring each nipple as you start taking uneven breaths, while one of my hands stray over towards China, who is without restraint sucking the lips of your vagina, until my fingers glide across her cheek causing her to look in my direction, with her keen eyes taking note of my firm erection, she begins trailing her way with kisses to your right breast, while I focus my attention on the ripe bud on the left. In the meanwhile you lay there with your right hand stroking my dick, while at the same time your fingers play with her clit. Then abandoning my post I seek out your femininity, making the transition to doggy style with all simplicity, as my dick probes your pussy with slow even strokes, your head tilts back as you arch your throat, with you deeply inhaling this sex filled air into your lungs, while in the background the stereo plays that track "I'm Sprung." As China assumes the position that you were previously in, she gazes into your eyes with a mischievous grin. In response you lean forward on your forearms and experiment with eating pussy for the first time, as your tongue shyly licks her clit until primal instinct takes over your mind, causing temporary insanity to take form, as your tongue thunders wildly about like a storm, her moans fill the room as her fingers thread through your hair. After fully returning the favor you finally come up for air. Then taking charge you get me to lie down on my back, while China straddles my face you straddle my shaft, with your hips grindin' up and down, and my tongue exploring

67

Chinatown, your coos and moans express fulfilled desires, as you both release your voices come together like a choirs. As ya'll continue to cum together like a symphony, your hands squeeze each other's breasts gently, followed by a slight pause in the mesmerizing motion of your hips, for the introduction of her tongue in between your lips. Then as your kiss winds down ya'll decide to trade places, except instead of riding me China's tongue sets out on a path that she traces, starting from my naval to the base of my shaft then up one side, as she reaches the tip her mouth tries to take the whole thing inside. After a few strokes her tongue snakes its way down the other side of my shaft, slowing just long enough to spread my cheeks and blow in my ass. Which causes me to jump at first from the unexpected entry, followed by my body reveling in the pleasure of her tongue licking around my hole gently. Just as I was beginning to think life couldn't get any better than this, you dismount my face and begin to deep throat my dick, causing me to violently explode and putting an arch in my spine, as a sweet rush of ecstasy completely blows my mind. Damn!

Sincerely yours,

Sin City

Dear Sunshine,

As I close my eyes my mind begins to drift, treasuring each moment we've shared like a priceless gift. Speaking of gifts as I prepare to describe one in a special way, thinking back on how you and I celebrated my birthday. As our plane begins its descent I take in the setting as I peer out the window, amazed by the stunning view of the neon lit desert city below, where lights shine so brightly the streets appear to be made of gold, with a beam shooting light out the tip of the Pyramid like the bat signal. Right then I'd almost be content to take in Vegas from the air, at least until I'm able to make out all those casinos down there. After collecting our luggage a cab takes us to our hotel, traveling the most scenic route I slowly become a victim of the city's magical spell. By the time we reach our destination my jaws are ready to hit the ground, from being amazed by all the sights and sounds. Gasping like tourists we walk up to the Hotel Bellagio, pausing to watch the extravagant front yard show with exploding volcanoes, along with sinking pirate ships, and at least a thousand fountains dancing in sync to music. Upon entering the lobby the casinos slot machines greet us, challenging us to a round or two as the gambling fever tries to reach us. Almost tempted to give in I force myself toward the check in desk. After settling into our suite we prepare for our adventurous quest. You end up changing outfits so you can wear your lucky shoes, while I dress in confidence cuz tonight I feel like I can't lose. Once we're ready we head out to the elevator and take it to the main floor, where we tour the cocktail lounges that are dressed in luxurious décor. Finding a corner booth and relaxing until the waitress comes

69

to take our order, not really all that hunger we settle on Grey Goose mixed with cranberry juice and snack on hors d'uerves. After another round of drinks we ask the waitress about the other hotels nearby. She then informs us about the joining walkways that seem suspended in the sky. Taking her advice we wide the elevator to the skywalks floor, and stroll across it to the Luxor, passing walls the shade of desert brown, with iris filled vases and Egyptian paintings all around. As we near the entrance an Egyptian dressed hostess beckons us inside and implores us to explore on our own, so we do and wind up staring at Pharaoh's throne, with all kinds of ancient artifacts and jewels in the chamber, and off to the right there's a passageway leading to a tomb where a mummy once lain there. After touring the museum we leave in search of action, entering the casino I'm taken back by all the gambling attractions. Not knowing where to start until I hear a loud "Ka-ching!" Coming from one of the numerous slot machines. We then find two unoccupied ones side by side, and make a bet on who is gonna win something first with only eleven tries. Coming so close but not close enough after the 21st round we finally give up and move onto something new, after a brief drinking intermission with a double shot of Hennessy for me and a strawberry daiquiri for you. From there we try our luck at the blackjack table and roulette wheel, as I look to the heavens for the right number to pick God shakes His head and says, "No Deal!" Running low on chips I go and reup for the last time, determined to beat the odds as a true gambler in my own mind, as I stare at my target as if we're in a wild west showdown, knowing that in the end one of us is gonna go down. Feeling confident I make my way over to the craps table, with years of playing in the streets when it came to winning I'm more than able. Which is what I do for the first 12 rounds, until greed sets in and my luck turns back around. Next thing I know I'm down to my last four chips, that's when you ask if you can try your hand at it. With a swinging for the fences attitude you decide to bet it all. My eyes become fixed on the table as you let the dice fall. Tumbling along until they magically stop on four and three, I let out a sigh and tell you to do your thing, as you continue to bet everything at one time, our winnings continue to soar and climb. Eventually others come up to the table and side bet on you to win, as you're repeatedly declared the winner again and again. Finally after making everyone else rich and doubling what we started off with, we cash in our chips and call it quits. Having done played against the odds and won we head back to the Bellagio to celebrate, not to mention open my present mmm... I can't wait.

To be continued

Sincerely yours,

Sin City Part 2

Dear Sunshine,

As we take our leave from the loud and flashy casino in route to our suite, we once again cross the skywalk with the world beneath our feet, leaving us feeling as if we're walking on air, as we near the Bellagio practically gliding there, with your bright beautiful smile stretching across your eloquent face, adding a brilliant glow to the already illuminated place. A glow that could compete with a cloudless afternoon sun, a glow that I will always remember for year to come. In the elevator now my mind wonders what all you got in store, as I catch the mischief in your eyes just before you press the red button stopping us between floors, with passion surging like lightning through our veins, our lips ravish each others as if they're untamed, along with hands searching, finding, and holding on for dear life, until the sudden crackle from the loud speaker asks "Is everything alright." After assuring the voice that everything is fine, we resume our descent with no interruptions this time. Following a few brief kisses along the way to our suite's door, we pause at the entrance as your gaze reaches the depths of my core, like a wild fire consuming my will to give in, as our lips meet my tongues probes your mouth again and again. This time there's a body to the voice, an old gray haired woman with a nametag that read Joyce. As we slip inside our room to escape her reprimanding glare, we laugh once inside at the thought of her crazed disapproving stare. After the laughter dies down our eyes meet and once gain I'm like and animal in heat. Sensing the untamed desire building you begin to step back in retreat, as I try to approach you exclaim "Wait I have a surprise!" and "This time you don't have to cover your eyes." Intrigued I allow you to guide me to the bed and obediently stay, as you gather your things, dim the lights, and head to the bathroom I wonder what game were fend to play. Anticipating its gonna be erotic I strip down to my birthday suit, as I settle back on the bed the door opens to a delicious view. With a seductive smile on your face you begin to sashay my way, as you sing your own version of "Happy Birthday." Nearing the bed I can clearly make out the creamy white icing and scattered sprinkles that cover your breasts, with a red bow replacing the triangle tufts of hair covering the rest. Then you tell me to make a wish and blow out the candle extended in your right hand, I reply "For what when its already come true" as I blow it out and place it on the night stand, as you offer me some of that all natural cake, my mouth greedily accepts as it savors the taste, while my arms wrap around your hips pulling you onto the plush bed, as I continue to devour your nipples as if my hunger can never be fed, you moan with delight as if off to heaven your spirit went, while my tongue trails down your body to unwrap my present. After carefully removing the bow I kiss the spot it once occupied, before my kisses drift down to that magical place in between your thighs, as your fingers go from running over my hair to tugging on my ears, while the fire burning inside begins to erupt your eyes well up with tears, As your muscles go from tense to relaxed, my tongue glides over your skin as it retraces its tracks, lingering at your breasts to finish off the icing that it missed, before it trails up your neck and my mouth slants over your lips. In the meanwhile your hands trace down my sides until they're caressing my cock, immediately our closed eyes spring open as they find each other's and lock. Our breath becoming ragged as you guide me home, making you the flesh of my flesh and the bone of my bone, as my slow thrusts turn into a driving piston, the sweat and saliva on your breasts begin to glisten, with your thighs tightly wrapped around my hips, grunts and moans escape our lips, my hands become interlaced with yours as our arms stretch above our heads, as the flames of passion begin to ignite and spread, full of blaze as we're consumed in ecstasy, while our hearts, bodies, and souls mix together like a recipe. Then as the flames slowly die down we lie there cuddled up tight, savoring each other's warmth as we turn in for the night.

Sincerely yours,

The Reckoning

Dear Sunshine,

Each and every morning I awaken with our history on my mind, as I try to unravel the mystery of our times, beginning with what really happened over 3 years ago, with the rhythm of the rhyme guiding my flow. After the first rendezvous on that warm sweet spring day, the saga continued as we stole moments of time until the end of May. Upon graduation it became easier to see each other, with us spending every moment possible together over the summer, in between my two jobs and me hustlin' on the side, as you went from cut friend status to a potential future bride. But being immature and in my prime I wasn't ready to slow down, so I ran the streets looking for chances to hoe around. From the present reflecting on the past that is something I aint proud of. Especially considering my main problem was being afraid of falling in love. However, that issue got put on the back burner as I continued to wild out, while living the fast lifestyle that rappers always rappin' about. 17 with my own car, crib, and rules you know I was living it up, along with the money, power, and respect how could I give it up. Yet through all the ups and downs you were always there, letting me know that no matter what you would always care, and love me whether times were thick or thin, and remain in my corner until the end. Well true to your word we made it through the summer and into the fall, with our relationship progressing to the point I was finally ready to give you my all. After cutting loose all the others I began working on changing my ways, with plans of going totally legit after my birthday, which was in the month of October four days before Halloween, and to celebrate the occasion my crew threw me a helluva party, that took place at a car & audio shop cinderalla'd into a club, stocked with mo alcoholic beverages than your average pub, with a local DJ spinning nothing but hits, as the ladies gyrate their luscious hips, while the hustlers work on gettin' their Mac on, you got other folks un the garage area gettin' their snack on. After all you know niggas always got the munchies, especially at a party where you got all you can smoke trees. Now in the back stereo soundproof room that was converted into the VIP, we sipped on champagne with strippers that aimed to please. But as willing as they were I had other things on my mind, specifically me and you spending some quality time. After making, my rounds I thank the host and step outside, where one of my niggas asked me for a ride. With his destination on the way it wasn't a big deal, so I quickly agreed then slid behind the wheel. As we cruised down 41A then turned on Peachers Mill Rd, I glanced in my rearview mirror to see that we were being followed by 5-0. Calmly I announce the fact and tell ole boy to play it cool, but that hardheaded nigga turned around like a fool. Almost simultaneously the light show began, followed by my passenger moving around frantically while saying in a panicked voice "Damn!" Me on the other hand I was straight chillin', having done retired from the game wasn't nothing to find from my dealings. As soon as I pulled into the Minit Mart and parked the Po-pos began to box me in, along with two other squad cars full of his friends. Then suddenly they exploded from their cars with guns trained on us, or should I say me cuz as he casually got out the car I knew I had been set up. Once it was all said and done a loaded .45, a QP, and an 8 Ball were miraculously found in my car. So needless to say I spent the rest of the evening behind bars. 7 months later I found myself in front of a bitter beer faced judge, who

76

looked me up and down with contempt as if he were holding a grudge, which must have been the case cuz as he sentenced me he revealed a smile so cold, while announcing "I hereby sentence you to 5 years without parole." Now from my present niche I look forward to that day of redemption, as I peer out the window in a hopeful condition, seeing you waiting for me day after day in the parking lot, always smiling regardless if the weather is cold or hot. Even from here I can see the glimmer in your eyes, that comforts my soul and causes my spirits to rise, which in turn replaces the turmoil in my mind with peace, as we both wait patiently for that day when I'm released. As the days turn into years our memories become a part of me, until reality sets in that it's all just part of a poets fantasy.

Sincerely yours,

City Councilman Richard Garrett has gained extensive business knowledge and negotiating skills as the Executive Director of the LEAP Organization. LEAP provides youth development services. As a licensed realtor for Keller Williams Realty, he is known for his tenacity, perseverance, honesty, and fairness. A proud APSU alum, Richard graduated with Honors with a Bachelors in Public Management.

Richard is a former active duty Marine, father of 4, and a husband with strong ties to the community. He is a graduate of Leadership Clarksville and Leadership CMCSS and is a member of Clarksville Rotary, Clarksville Area Ministerial Association, Chamber of Commerce, Clarksville Association of Realtors Public Relations & Charity Relations Committees, and Clarksville Community Partners Group.

Liberated Publishing Inc.
1860 Wilma Rudolph Blvd
Clarksville, TN 37040
info@liberatedpublishing.com
931-378-0500

www.LiberatedPublishing.com

www.ingramcontent.com/pod-product-compliance
Lightning Source LLC
Chambersburg PA
CBHW071716140626
46557CB00011B/727